The Boy Who Loved Bananas

Written by
George Elliott

Illustrated by
Andrej Krystoforski

Kids Can Press

Matthew loved the elephants and he loved the crocodiles.
He loved the giraffes and he loved the polar bears.

But of all the animals in the Metro Zoo, Matthew loved the monkeys the most.

Matthew laughed himself silly when he watched the monkeys at feeding time. They would climb and tumble, wrestle and swing. And while they played, they would devour dozens of ripe bananas.

"How come monkeys eat so many bananas?" Matthew asked the monkey keeper.

"I suppose it's because they LOVE bananas!" the monkey keeper replied.

"Hmmm," said Matthew.

That evening, Matthew would not eat his dinner.
"But pizza is your favorite," said his mother.
"Bananas are my favorite now," said Matthew.
"I thought you hated bananas," said his father.
"I LOVE BANANAS!" insisted Matthew.

A little while later, Matthew excused himself from the table. Nine banana peels lay on his plate.

"I think something strange is going on," said Matthew's mother.

"I think we need more bananas," said Matthew's father.

For the next two weeks, Matthew ate nothing but bananas —

banana bread,

banana muffins,

banana chips,

banana pie,

banana splits,

banana milkshakes,

banana pudding,

banana soufflé,

banana tarts

and even banana casseroles.

Every day his father asked, "Wouldn't you like a nice hamburger?"
Every day his mother asked, "How about a delicious bowl of
spaghetti?"
"MORE BANANAS, PLEASE!" Matthew always answered.

One day, Matthew was at the zoo with his parents watching the monkeys as they romped, tussled and did somersaults and back flips. He had just finished eating his fourteenth banana of the day.

"Mmmm-mm!" said Matthew. "I LOVE bananas!"

Suddenly, Matthew felt a tingling sensation.

"Strange," he said, scratching the seat of his shorts. "I feel itchy. Maybe I'd better eat another banana."

Matthew quickly peeled and ate his fifteenth banana.

"I still feel itchy," he said, scratching under his baseball cap.

"Maybe you're getting a rash," said his mother.

"Maybe you're allergic to bananas," said his father.

Matthew scratched and scratched and scratched.

He scratched his itchy head.

He scratched his itchy tummy.

He scratched his itchy back.

And he scratched his itchy knees.

Matthew itched and scratched and itched and scratched until, all of a sudden, something went ...

KABLOOEY!

… and Matthew TRANSMOGRIFIED into a hairy little monkey.

"My goodness!" said Matthew's mother.

"My gracious!" said Matthew's father.

"HURRAY!" said Matthew.

The other monkeys jumped up and down. They shrieked and pointed at Matthew.

A crowd started to gather.

"Hey! There's a monkey on the loose!" someone yelled.

Within moments, three zookeepers with big nets surrounded Matthew.

"WAIT!" yelled Matthew's father. "That's not a monkey! THAT'S MY SON!"

"Your son?!" the three zookeepers asked, scratching their heads.

"Maybe you should take him to a doctor," said the first zookeeper.

"Maybe you should take him to a veterinarian," said the second zookeeper.

"Maybe you should take him to a barber!" said the third zookeeper.

"We're taking him home!" Matthew's mother and father said.

Over the next few weeks, Matthew's parents tried everything they could think of to turn Matthew back into a boy —

hypnotism,

acupuncture,

yoga,

foot massages,

psychotherapy

and even mud baths.

Matthew visited seven doctors, six veterinarians, five herbalists, four chiropractors, three animal trainers, two psychiatrists and even one psychic.

They all came to the same conclusion.

"Matthew *likes* being a monkey," they said. "He will stop being a monkey when he *wants* to stop being a monkey."

Matthew did not want to stop being a monkey. He was having oodles of fun climbing monkey bars, swinging through trees and shinnying up flagpoles.

The boys and girls at school laughed themselves silly watching Matthew perform.

Soon, all the kids at school began devouring bananas at lunchtime.

Even the school principal was secretly gobbling bananas by the dozen.

One sunny Saturday at the Metro Zoo, Matthew and his parents were passing the African elephant pavilion on their way to the monkey pavilion when a big bull elephant wrapped its trunk around a tree and pulled it right out of the ground.

"Holy guacamole!" exclaimed Matthew.

"The African elephant is the strongest land animal on the planet," the elephant keeper said.

"Really?" asked Matthew. "What do elephants eat?"

"This one sure likes peanuts," said the elephant keeper.

"Hmmm," said Matthew.

That evening, Matthew would not eat his dinner.
"I don't feel like bananas," he said.
Matthew's mother and father jumped for joy.
"What would you like to eat?" asked Matthew's mother.
"Beef stew?" asked Matthew's father. "Lasagna? Macaroni and cheese?"

Matthew smiled a mischievous monkey smile.
"I want ... PEANUTS!" he said.

For Matthew Elliott, the real boy who
loved bananas — G.E.

For my family — A.K.

Kids Can Press acknowledges the financial support of the Government of Ontario, through the Ontario Media
Development Corporation's Ontario Book Initiative; the Ontario Arts Council; the Canada Council for the Arts;
and the Government of Canada, through the BPIDP, for our publishing activity.

Published in Canada by
Kids Can Press Ltd.
29 Birch Avenue
Toronto, ON M4V 1E2

Published in the U.S. by
Kids Can Press Ltd.
2250 Military Road
Tonawanda, NY 14150

www.kidscanpress.com

The artwork in this book was rendered in pen and watercolor.
The text is set in Kabel Book.

Edited by Jennifer Stokes
Designed by Julia Naimska
Printed and bound in China

The hardcover edition of this book is smyth sewn casebound.
The paperback edition of this book is limp sewn with a drawn-on cover.

CM 05 0 9 8 7 6 5 4 3 2
CM PA 06 0 9 8 7 6 5 4 3 2 1

National Library of Canada Cataloguing in Publication Data

Elliott, George, 1964–
        The boy who loved bananas / written by George Elliott ; illustrated by Andrej Krystoforski.

ISBN-13: 978-1-55337-744-3 (bound)   ISBN-10: 1-55337-744-3 (bound)
ISBN-13: 978-1-55453-119-6 (pbk.)   ISBN-10: 1-55453-119-5 (pbk.)

I. Krystoforski, Andrej, 1943– II. Title.

PS8559.L5445B69 2005   jC813'.6   C2004-904767-1

Kids Can Press is a *corus* Entertainment company